Who Will
WEAR
the
CROWN?

ISBN 978-1-63885-508-8 (Paperback)
ISBN 978-1-63885-510-1 (Hardcover)
ISBN 978-1-63885-509-5 (Digital)

Copyright © 2022 Ellen Mongan and Elle Young
All rights reserved
First Edition

All scripture references are from the New American Bible Revised Edition.

All rights reserved. No part of this publication may be reproduced, distributed, or transmitted in any form or by any means, including photocopying, recording, or other electronic or mechanical methods without the prior written permission of the publisher. For permission requests, solicit the publisher via the address below.

Covenant Books
11661 Hwy 707
Murrells Inlet, SC 29576
www.covenantbooks.com

Who Will WEAR the CROWN?

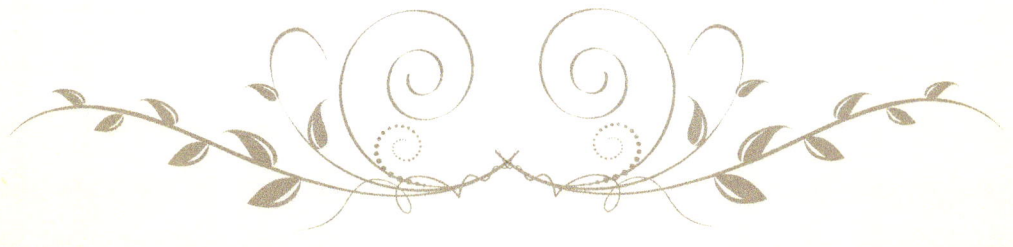

Ellen Mongan and Elle Young

"Once upon a time, in a heavenly land very far away, there lived a king whose name was Jesus. He ruled His kingdom with both love and truth. Jesus was all-knowing, all-powerful, and all good, the One True God. He could see into the hearts of all. If a heart was turned toward Him, they could ask Him to become the King of their heart. His love was freely given and must be freely received to those who choose Him."

"This is my favorite bedtime story, Mommy. I chose King Jesus to be King of my heart too."

"Elle Grace, that is an excellent choice. I know you chose Jesus as King of your heart," said Mommy. "I am so proud of you." Elle's ears perked up as Mommy continued the bedtime story, "All who knew Jesus lived their lives for Him. That was how they showed Him they love Him. Jesus loved everyone best!"

Elle popped in with, "Mommy, Mommy, I love Jesus best too."

Mommy grinned as she replied, "Elle, yes, you do."

Elle's smile seemed to grow an inch wider. It always seemed to do that when Mommy talked about Jesus. "Tell me more, Mommy," Elle Grace pleaded.

Mommy read more. "Jesus loved His people so much that He made a journey to earth to show them how to get to their heavenly home. Even though the earth was far, far away, His love for them made it seem like a twinkle of an eye. Then Jesus began to teach the people on earth His way to love Him and to love one another. Not everyone liked Jesus or His Way and His Truth because they wanted their way and their truth. Jesus was very sad because He could not fill them with His Spirit of love. Jesus would not make them choose Him because that would take away their free will. 'For God so loved the world that He gave His only Son, so that everyone who believes in Him might not perish but might have eternal life' (John 3:16)."

"We cannot wait, can we? We cannot wait to get to heaven! Right, Mommy?"

"You are so right, Elle Grace." Mommy thought Elle had fallen asleep, but she was listening to every word.

Jesus told them to tell everyone the good news of how to get to His Kingdom of love. Jesus's friends told everyone they met. They wrote all Jesus taught them in a book called the Bible. The Bible tells us all about Jesus's life on earth and teaches us how to live for King Jesus. People who love Him cannot wait to be happy one day with Him in heaven. Just like in the times that Jesus walked the earth, today we are given the same invitation. Jesus calls to all, "Come follow me."

"Do you hear Him calling your name?"

"I do, Mommy, I hear Him call my name."

"Have you answered His invitation?"

"Yes, Lord! Yes, Lord! Yes, yes, yes!" Elle started singing.

Mommy joined in. "Yes, yes, yes, Lord."

The homes in heaven are reservation only. Jesus gives us the invitation while we live on the earth. Whosoever calls upon the name of Jesus and asks Him to be the King of their heart will become His children, and live one day in His heavenly home.

"That is not all!"

Elle interrupted with, "This is my favorite part, Mommy."

Whoever follows Jesus and asks Him to be King of their heart will live by the law of love and one day receive a crown. Jesus will place this crown on their heads Himself. The crown would be made especially for them, so it fits their head perfectly. A jewel is placed on their crown each time a kind deed is done out of love for Jesus. King Jesus places various jewels in the crowns: rubies, emeralds, and even sapphires. No one can see the crown or the jewels; however, those who know Jesus know they are there. They trust Jesus, their King, because he was a God of truth.

Each time the children do a good deed, they can almost see their crown sparkling. They imagine King Jesus smiling at them, and they always smile back at Him. Many children wanted King Jesus to place a crown on their heads. They would read their Bibles and practice good deeds, and practice virtue. Once they received their crowns, they tried to do all things out of love for Jesus and not just receive the jewels for their crown; that was how much they loved Him. They knew that when they got to heaven, their crown would shine for the glory of their King, Jesus. It is in heaven that all things invisible on earth would be visible for all to see. In heaven, Jesus would be crowned with many crowns. Every knee will bow as the crowns are placed at the feet of Jesus. Every tongue would confess, "Jesus Christ is Lord." Oh, what a glorious day it will be to meet Jesus face to face! They could not wait! They longed to live in their heavenly home.

"Elle Grace," Mommy added, "Jesus takes care of His children like Mommy and Daddy care for you. When they are sad, Jesus comforts them. When they are wrong, Jesus corrects them. When they call upon His name, He answers them. You can hear Jesus talk to you, not in a loud voice but rather in a still, small voice heard in the silence of your heart."

Every time Mommy read the story about the King's crown, Elle Grace learned something new. She could not wait until King Jesus placed a crown on her head. Every day she tried to do at least one good deed. She tried to obey Mommy and Daddy right away, and sometimes with a smile. When her friends came over, she shared her toys and took turns being first. She rarely forgot to say her prayers.

Elle Grace wanted to have a crown full of jewels to please her friend Jesus, the King of her heart. One day, Elle looked in the mirror and was sure she saw her crown. "Mommy, Mommy!" she called, "King Jesus has placed a crown on my head, and I think I can see it."

Mommy came running into Elle's bedroom. She smiled and said, "Why, Elle Grace, I think I see your crown too. Look, it fits your head perfectly, just like in the story."

"Mommy, Mommy, the story is true! I felt King Jesus place my crown on my head Himself." Elle smiled her best smile even though her two front teeth were missing. "Mommy, do you think that King Jesus is smiling at me?"

"Yes, Elle! Yes, Elle, yes, yes, yes!" Mommy responded by singing their favorite song but changing the words a bit.

Elle ran out of her bedroom, holding her crown on both sides.

Lauren, her sister, looked at her with admiration, saying, "Elle, your crown is so beautiful!"

Elle proudly took Lauren's hand, and together they went looking for their baby sister, Ava, to tell her all about the crown. Elle, Lauren, and Ava also told the good news to daddy, nana, papa, and all her friends. The next day at school, Elle Grace told everyone she knew the story of the King's Crown. All the children wanted a crown of their own from King Jesus, everyone except Mean Thomas.

Thomas did not believe that Elle had a crown. He never heard of the land far away called heaven. Mean Thomas began to make fun of Elle Grace while all the children were listening to her. "Where is your crown, Elle Grace? I don't see one on your head. You are making up this whole story, Elle Grace!" Thomas mocked. Elle did not respond. She knew that the crown was real. She just sat still and prayed. She pictured Jesus putting a jewel in her crown for being patient with Thomas. Thomas continued to tease Elle, saying, "Elle Grace, one day I am going to snatch your crown and place it on my head instead." Elle held on to her crown with all her might and began to cry.

When Elle got home, she told Mommy and Daddy the whole story. Daddy picked her up, placed her on his lap, and gave her a big hug.

"Daddy, Daddy, Thomas made fun of me in front of my friends. He does not believe that I have a crown from King Jesus with sparkling jewels. He does not even believe in the land far away called heaven."

Daddy looked into Elle's eyes and replied, "Elle, I do not think that Thomas knows how much Jesus loves him. He wants to snatch your crown because he is jealous. You see, if Thomas knew Jesus, He would love Him too." Daddy dried Elle's tears, and she began to smile again.

Mommy, who was standing at the door, heard everything and said, "We must all pray for Thomas to get to know Jesus. Then Thomas will want Him to be King of his heart too."

Daddy said, "One more thing, Elle Grace. Jesus wants you to be a good example so you can lead Thomas to Him."

Mommy agreed, "Yes, Elle, we must all be good examples and pray."

Elle hopped off Daddy's lap, hugging Mommy and Daddy at the same time. Then placing her hands on her hips, she shouted, "I'll show that Mean Thomas an example or two!"

"Whoa, Elle Grace, hold your horses. There will be no name-calling in our home."

Elle hung her head down. "Sorry, Daddy. I guess that was not being a good example, was it?"

"It is all right, Elle. We are all sinners. Do you see why we need Jesus to be King of our hearts?"

"Yes, sir!" Elle agreed.

Elle could not wait to get to school the next day so she could see Thomas. She was determined to be a good example and to show Thomas how much Jesus loved him. She really wanted Thomas to love him too. Every day she would pray for Thomas. When she saw him, she would tell him all about her friend Jesus. It seemed to Elle Grace that the more she prayed and talked to Thomas about Jesus, the meaner he treated her. However, that did not stop Elle. She knew that Jesus was real, and so was the King's crown. Elle's heart was full of Jesus's love, so she kept on praying and being a good example.

Mean Thomas was so mad that he threatened her. "Elle Grace," he shouted, "one day, I am going to snatch your crown of jewels off your head and put it on my head instead!"

Elle was about to shake her finger at Thomas and say, "No siree, Thomas, the crown is mine, and the jewels are for me." Instead, she paused and remembered what Jesus did when people were mean to Him. "Thomas," she said, holding her crown on tight with both hands, "I am going to pray that Jesus will put a crown on your head that is just your size." Even though Elle did the right thing, Thomas's words still hurt her heart. Elle fought back her tears.

When they were sharing around the dinner table that evening about the best part of their day, Elle said, "I prayed for Thomas to get a crown." Mommy and Daddy were so proud. Lauren cheered, "Way to go, Elle!" Ava said, "That is just what Jesus would do!" Elle smiled with delight.

Sadly, when the family shared the worst part of their day, Elle's smile turned upside down into a frown. Elle began to cry. "Thomas mocked me," she sobbed. Tears filled her eyes as she related, "Mean Thomas does not believe I have a crown, or there is a King Jesus. Thomas said that he is going to snatch my crown away."

Mommy got up from the table, put her arms around Elle Grace, and hugged her. "Princess," she said, "it was good you prayed for Thomas. He must not know how much Jesus loves Him. That is why he wants to steal your crown." Mommy dried Elle's tears as she reassured her, "Besides, Elle, even if Thomas steals your crown, it won't fit his head. Your crown was made just for you. It fits your head perfectly. Elle, that is how much Jesus loves you."

At that very moment, Daddy walked over to Elle to say, "Jesus loves everyone this much!" He put both His arms around her and hugged her tight. Quicker than a wink, Elle found herself flying in the air as Daddy twirled her round and round.

Elle giggled and held on tight as she said, "Daddy, yes, He does! Jesus loves everyone, even Mean Thomas!"

"Elle Grace," Daddy replied in his authoritative voice, "name-calling is not allowed in this house. No more saying Mean Thomas. How about we call him Magnificent Thomas? Because that is just what he will be when he meets the King and is filled with Jesus's love."

Lauren and Ava began to sing, "Jesus loves me—this I know, for the Bible tells me so!" Then they jumped up and down, shouting, "Daddy, Daddy, can we have a turn?"

Daddy put Elle down, opened his arms wide, and gave a group hug. "I have three princesses to twirl. Now let's take turns, ladies."

"Me first, Daddy!" said Ava.

"Me first, Daddy!" said Lauren.

"Me last, Daddy, because I already had my turn," said Elle.

"What a good attitude, Elle!" encouraged Mommy. "I can see the jewels in your crown shining brighter than the gleam in your eye, Elle!"

"Thank you, Mommy!" said Elle, politely remembering her manners. "One day, Jesus will give Thomas eyes to see the jewels in my crown showing my love for Jesus!" boasted Elle.

Elle continued to pray day after day for Thomas to know Jesus. She knew if he knew Jesus, he would love Jesus and would want to serve Jesus. Then Jesus would place a crown on Thomas's head that would fit perfectly. Jewels would be placed in his crown as he served King Jesus. Elle wanted this for Thomas more than Thomas wanted it for himself. She could not wait to see Thomas become Magnificent Thomas.

One day, something horrible happened! Elle was talking to her friends Ashlyn Hope, Maggie, Brookie, and Audrey Love about Jesus. Thomas snuck up behind her and snatched her crown. Then away Thomas ran shouting, "I told you so! I told you so! I told you I would steal your precious crown, Princess Elle Grace." Then Thomas said, "Look, Elle, I captured your crown, and now it will be mine forever. I am going to put your crown with all the jewels on my head." Elle turned around, took one look at Thomas, and ran after him. Though tears were streaming down her cheeks and Elle could barely catch her breath, she ran her fastest and was determined to rescue her stolen crown. Elle ran, but Thomas was faster! Soon he was out of her sight. Elle did not know what to do, so she stopped and began to pray. She knew that King Jesus was all-knowing. She knew He would help her find Thomas, rescue her crown, and place it back on her head where it belonged.

Thomas was very proud of himself. Not only had he snatched Elle's precious crown, but he had outrun her. He was hiding in the boys' bathroom, where he knew she would never find him. Thomas smiled at himself in the mirror as he placed the crown upon his head. Thomas was sure it would fit just fine. Then something unexpected happened. What do you think it was?

Did Elle find Thomas? Did the crown disappear before his eyes? Did Thomas change his mind and decide to return the crown to Elle? Did the teacher find Thomas? Did the crown fit just fine after all?

No, Elle did not find Thomas! No, the crown did not disappear before his eyes! No, Thomas did not return the crown. No, the teacher did not find him either.

Surprisingly, as Thomas placed Elle's crown upon his head, it slipped all the way down to his neck. The sparkling jewels surrounded Thomas's neck like a necklace. It was as if the crown was trying to give Thomas a message. Every time the jewels sparkled before his eyes in the mirror, he was reminded of all the times he was mean to Elle. He remembered each time Elle repaid his bad behavior with a kind deed. Thomas stopped and took a good look in the mirror. It was the first time that Thomas came face-to-face with himself. Thomas did not like what he saw. Tears began to flow from his eyes—tears of repentance. A desire to know Jesus for himself was growing in his heart. He thought that stealing the crown would make him happy, but all the crown of jewels did was remind him of how mean he had been, especially to Jesus's friend Elle.

This time, Thomas was the one who was surprised. He knew the crown was real. He knew Jesus was real. In a moment, in a twinkle of an eye, he knew all that Elle said about Jesus and the crown of jewels was absolutely, positively true. Thomas looked at himself in the mirror eyeball to eyeball and liked what he saw, a boy with a heart for Jesus. As he was about to jump for joy, he realized he was not alone. It was the Good-Deeders who had come to Elle's aid. They came to rescue the crown and return it to the rightful owner, Princess Elle Grace.

Did the Good-Deeders make fun of Thomas because he had Elle's crown around his neck that looked like a necklace? No, they were the Good-Deeders, who do what is right because they follow Jesus. Did the Good-Deeders shout at Thomas and snatch the crown off Thomas's neck? No, they were the Good-Deeders.

So, what did the Good-Deeders do? One Good-Deeder gave Thomas a hug and said, "It is okay, Thomas. Elle has already forgiven you!" Another Good-Deeder grabbed a tissue from his pocket and dried Thomas's tears without saying a word. The third Good-Deeder compassionately explained, "Thomas, that crown is way too big for you. It was made to only fit the head of Princess Elle Grace. The jewels on that crown were chosen by the King for Elle when she served Him." Tears welled up in Thomas's eyes. The Good-Deeders knew how much Thomas wanted to know, love, and serve Jesus. They reassured him by saying, "If you make Jesus the King of your heart, He will place a crown on your head that was made to fit perfectly. Jesus will set before you a life of good deeds that He has selected for you to do through His amazing grace. These good deeds will fit your gifts and talents perfectly. Your life will become a thank-you in return for what He has done for you. He died for you, and now you can gratefully live for Him. Thomas, Jesus loves everyone best. Do you want to make Him King of your heart?"

Now, Thomas smiled. All he ever wanted to do was to have Jesus love Him best. The Good-Deeders helped him see how he could do that. It really wasn't about a crown of jewels or jealousy of Elle all along. No, Thomas desperately wanted to be loved by Jesus. Now Thomas could not wait to give Elle back her crown and to tell Elle the good news of how God had turned his heart toward Him, how she was right all along, how Jesus is real! Jesus truly fills your heart with love when you ask Him to be King of your heart. Thomas knew it was true because he could even feel Jesus inside his heart. He had met Elle's King when he looked himself face-to-face in the mirror and did not lie about what He saw. God changed his heart when Thomas was ready to face the truth about himself. We all need Jesus, our Savior, to die for our sins; we all need Jesus to fill our hearts with His love.

With one Good-Deeder on Thomas's right side and the other Good-Deeder on the left side, the three walked arm in arm back towards Elle. The third Good-Deeder was carefully carrying Elle's crown of jewels. Elle saw them coming and began to sprint toward them. She knew from the way that Thomas was hanging his head that he was sorry. Elle blurted out, "I forgive you, Thomas!" before Thomas even had a chance to apologize. "Thomas, I prayed for you to love Jesus and to follow Him with all your heart."

Elle thanked the Good-Deeders for helping Thomas and for bringing back her crown. Thomas began to tell Elle about the miracle that just happened in his heart. Now it was Thomas who could not stop talking about Jesus the King and how He filled his heart with love. Elle was very excited! "Thomas, you have changed. You talk different, and you even look different. I know that you have made Jesus the King of your heart. One day He will place a crown on your head, and it will fit your head perfectly. One day He will fill your crown with jewels that will shine before men for the good deeds you have done through His amazing grace. One day we will be happy with Him in heaven. We will place our crown of jewels at the feet of Jesus because we did the good deeds for His glory alone."

The Good-Deeders and Elle proclaimed together these words,

> We will cry, "Holy, Holy, Holy,
> Lord God Almighty,
> Who Was
> And Who Is
> And Who Is to Come."

Then the Good-Deeders and Elle and Thomas joined hands together in a circle, singing and dancing.

> Crown Him with many crowns,
> The Lamb upon the throne.

Elle added her own verse, saying, "We want to crown Him with many crowns full of jewels. Right, Good-Deeders?"

"Amen," they all replied, even Thomas.

Slowly and carefully, Princess Elle Grace placed the crown back upon her head. The Good-Deeders made sure it was on just right. A permanent smile reappeared on her face, which held the joy and love in her heart from knowing King Jesus. "Thanks, Good-Deeders," Elle said.

The Good-Deeders responded with, "Only Jesus takes a bow. Right, Elle Grace?"

"That's right, friends," Elle replied. Then Elle said in her most mature voice, "Come on, Good-Deeders, there is work to be done. We need to tell all the Good News. Jesus loves everyone best!"

"Yes, he does," Thomas said in agreement. "But you must make Him King of your heart and let Him fill you with His love." He added.

"That is the Good News, Thomas," Elle proclaimed. "Now, Magnificent Thomas, go tell the world!"

The End

The Invitation

Not only did Thomas meet Jesus that day, but also He filled Thomas's heart with His love. Jesus placed a crown upon his head that fit Thomas just fine when Thomas decided to join the Good-Deeders in living a life of virtue thru His amazing grace. The angels in heaven rejoiced that day because Thomas gave his life and his heart to Jesus.

How about you? Jesus wants to be King of your heart too. If you get to know Him, I promise you will love Him. If you love Him, you will want to serve Him. If you serve Him, you will be happy one day in heaven with Him. What are you waiting for, boys and girls? Do you want Jesus to be King of your heart and fill you with His love and with His amazing grace? What are you waiting for? Ask Him to be King of your heart. He always says yes; He loves you all best! He died for you.

Now, just like Elle did in the story, go forth with a life of good works. Tell the Good News to all you meet. One day Jesus will place a crown on your head. I know it will fit just fine; it will be made for your head alone. He will fill your crown with jewels for His glory alone.

Let your light shine before men so that they can see your good works and give glory to your Father in heaven. Fill that crown for His glory and shine as a good example in this world for Jesus. Now applaud God! Never forget, only Jesus takes a bow!

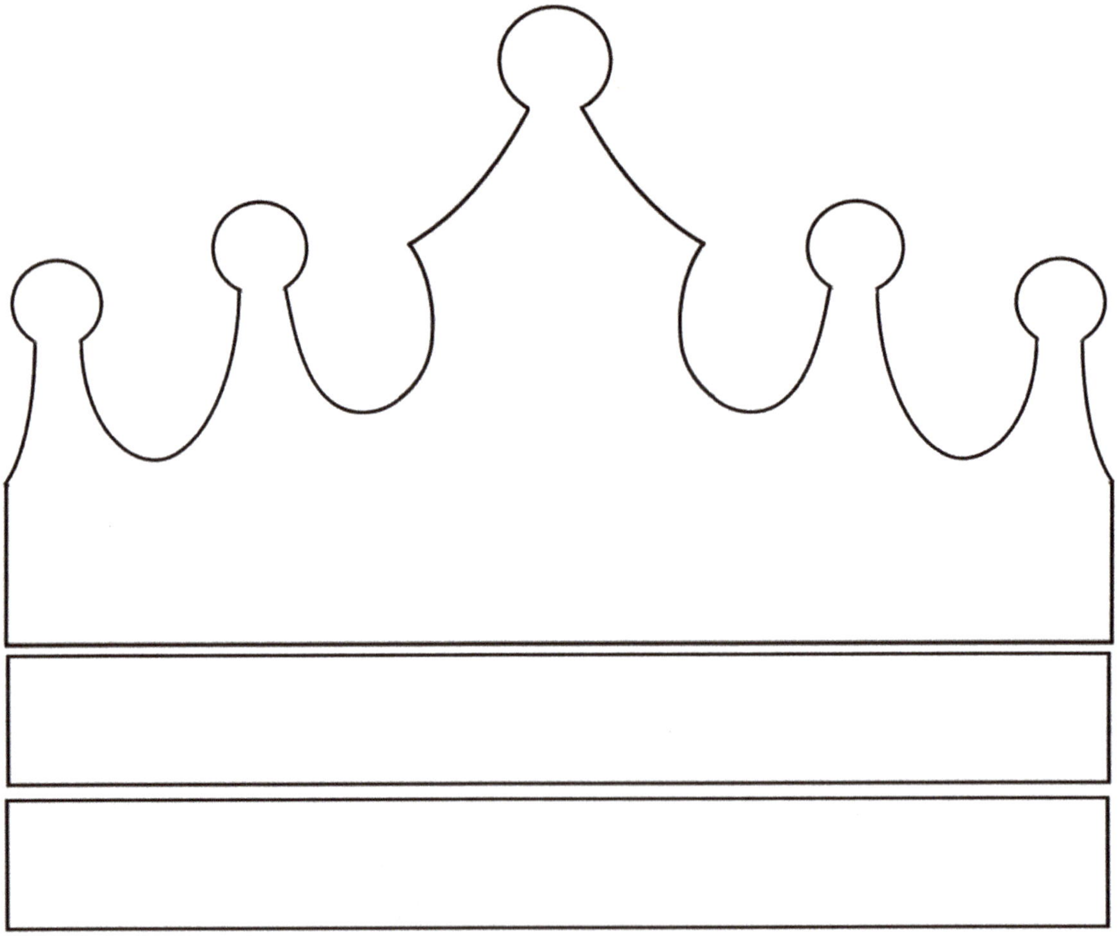

40

About the Co Author

Elle Young is attending Sacred Heart High School and is on the cheerleading squad. She enjoys family, friends, and social media.

Elle is not just an ordinary teenager; she is a creative genius. At a very young age she collaborated with her Nana, Ellen Mongan, to write "Who Will Wear the Crown?

This book will be an inspiration to all. To those aspiring authors out there you are never too old, nor too young to write a masterpiece.

About the Author

Ellen Mongan hosts three podcasts, *WOW MOM*, *Deacon and Dear, and Take 5*. She is a Christian author and speaker. Her book, *WOW MOM: A Walk with God*, was published by Covenant Books, Inc. Ellen writes a monthly faith column for the *Augusta Chronicle* newspaper. She is also a monthly contributor to *Catholic Mom*. She has blogged for *Women of Grace*. She is the founder of Little Pink Dress Ministry and Sisters in Christ. She has spoken on radio and television.

Ellen Mongan has been married forty-seven years to Deacon Patrick Mongan, MD. They have seven children, of whom six are married, a baby in heaven, and fourteen grandchildren. The vocation of wife and mother led her to her ministry. This is the most important role of all.

Ellen goes where God calls her to go and does what He asks her to do through His grace. Invite her to speak at your church, women's club, or mom's group. Her website is www.ellenmongan.com.

CPSIA information can be obtained
at www.ICGtesting.com
Printed in the USA
BVHW021553021122
650901BV00002B/12